Book One

of the

TRAVELS with ZOZO
SERIES

by A. J. Atlas
illustrated by Anne Zimanski

Welcome, Readers!

Before you get started, I thought you might like to know a few interesting things about the *Travels with Zozo...*® series. First of all, the stories are set in real places, so the illustrations you'll see try to show the actual landscapes, plants, and animals found in those locations. Second, the scientific, cultural, and historical elements you'll read about are also as accurate as possible. I hope this knowledge makes the books even more enjoyable for you.

For this story, the setting is Admiralty Island, Alaska, in the United States of America.

In a few parts of the story, a teeny bit more creativity and imagination was added. Most of it will be quite obvious, like the bear disguised inside a hollow tree who steals sandwiches. (That makes me laugh every time I see it!) Other, less obvious, elements that are not 100% accurate include the following:

- Bears don't cry. The only animal known to produce emotional tears and cry are humans. Some animals' eyes can tear in response to eye irritations or allergies but not joy, sadness, pain, grief, or other emotions.

- A park ranger and a guide accompany all groups on Admiralty Island. They are not described in the story, but they are an important part of keeping the land, animals, and visitors safe from harm.

- Bears should not be approached, even though Zozo does. It is not safe to go near or try to touch unknown animals.

For the most part, the rest of the information I have presented is accurate and, in my opinion, super interesting! Here are a few more fun facts:

- Admiralty Island is an island located in southern Alaska, near the state capital city of Juneau. It is a coastal temperate rainforest and home to more brown bears than live in the whole lower 48 states combined. It is estimated that 1,600 brown bears live there.

- Hibernation — bears can stay in their dens to avoid cold weather and lack of available food for as long as five to eight months. Originally thought to be an extended form of sleep, current research suggests this period of minimal activity relates to a lowered metabolic state.

And one last thing, one word with a pronunciation that might be new to you is Tarrak — taa-RAHK. It is the Inuit word for shadow.

— AJA

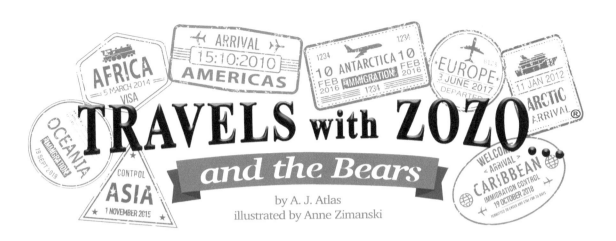

TRAVELS with ZOZO
and the Bears

by A. J. Atlas
illustrated by Anne Zimanski

IMAGINON
BOOKS

Zozo was a hoppity,

floppity,

huggable,

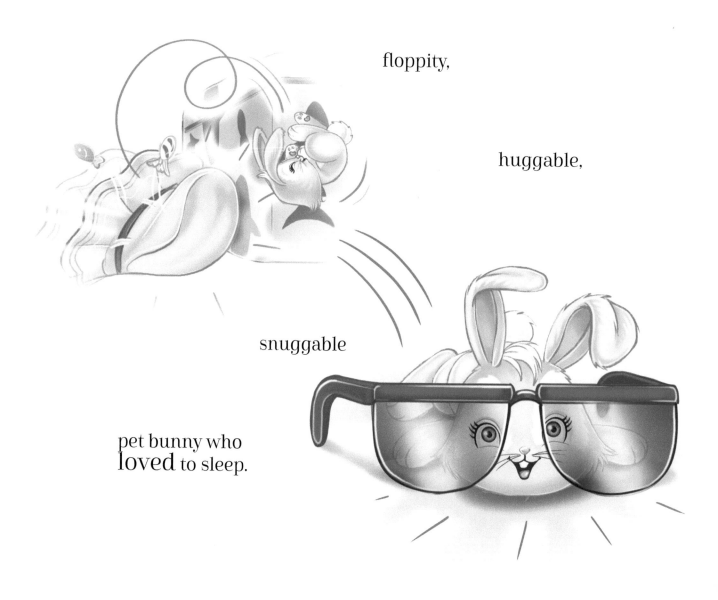

snuggable

pet bunny who **loved** to sleep.

She lived with a fun, on-the-run family of four who loved to travel. Together, they crisscrossed the world sharing adventures and making new friends.

Zozo and her family had traveled on vacation to see bears in the wild. A floatplane had brought them partway to their destination. Now sea kayaks would take them across a calm bay to a large island wilderness full of bears.

"I can't wait to see what the bears will be doing," said Zozo's seven-year-old brother, Benji, as they neared the island.

"Some might be exploring new places, like us," said Zozo's four-year-old sister, Jazz. Then, with a quick wink to Zozo, she continued, "Of course, *our bunny* is the best, but bears are great too! They're clever, strong, good at catching fish, and..."

As Jazz spoke, Zozo felt anticipation building inside her from the bottom of her paws to the tippy-top of her ears.

Thud, thud, thud. The pounding of heavy feet came from the tree line just beyond the beach.

Suddenly, three young brown bears broke through the trees and onto the beach.

Amazing! Zozo thought, watching the bears wrestling and rolling and bouncing and pouncing on each other. Their playfulness made Zozo wonder what fun other bears might be having.

Soon the bears moved off the beach and into the nearby river. Zozo and her family landed their kayaks and began hiking inland in search of more bears. They planned to spend the whole day hiking one long trail along the river and back again.

"Keep looking. There are sure to be more," Dad said, leading the group.

Everyone glanced left and right as they walked. But the dense rainforest made it hard to see animals. Though Zozo looked around a while from the top pocket of Benji's backpack, she was unable to see any bears. Like most little ones, she soon began to feel sleepy. It didn't take long before her tiny muscles relaxed and her eyelids began to feel heavy.

Zozo awoke in a treehouse in the woods. It was hidden high above the rainforest path, yet it was close to the river. This way, they could see the bears from a safe distance.

"Look at all the bears!" Mom said to her excited family.

For a long time, they watched different bears come and go.

A momma bear playing with her two cubs came along. A few big bears walked by alone.

Some bears ate blueberries from bushes near the river's edge. Many others caught fish in their mouths as they walked in the water.

Zozo and her family all wanted to stay and watch longer, but it was getting late. So instead, they headed back down the trail to the kayaks, hoping to see more bears along the way.

When everyone stopped for a rest and a snack, Zozo hopped out of Benji's backpack and nibbled on a wild blueberry. She liked how juicy and sweet it was. She leaned into the bush to get another and heard a sniffle and a small voice mumble, "Have you seen my brothers?"

Curious who was there, Zozo pushed her head into the bushes. Nestled into them was a young brown bear. Crushed blueberries covered his face, and tears filled his eyes.

"Maybe," Zozo said, surprised she was actually meeting a real bear, "we've seen many bears today."

"They left me behind," the bear said, more tears filling his eyes.

Zozo said, "Let's see...first, when we arrived on the beach, we saw three young bears tackling each other—"

"That's them!" interrupted the bear. "I'm the only young bear in this part of Alaska with three siblings. Most bears only have one or two. Where are they? Which beach?"

Zozo shrugged, not knowing the name of where they'd been. "We're going there now. I can show you."

"Okay!" the bear said as he wiped tears from his eyes. Seeming more cheerful, he shoveled a final few berries into his mouth. "On the way, let's play hide-and-go-seek," he said. "I'm super good at it! My momma named me Tarrak, which means *shadow*, because I'm just like a shadow in the woods. You'll see. Cover your eyes and count to ten, and I'll go hide. Wave when you see me, and I'll hide again."

Tarrak lumbered off into the rainforest. He looked back over his shoulder and joked, "Now watch as I make like a tree and leave!"

Zozo giggled. She hopped into Benji's backpack, closed her eyes, and began counting to ten. "1...2...3...4...5...6..."

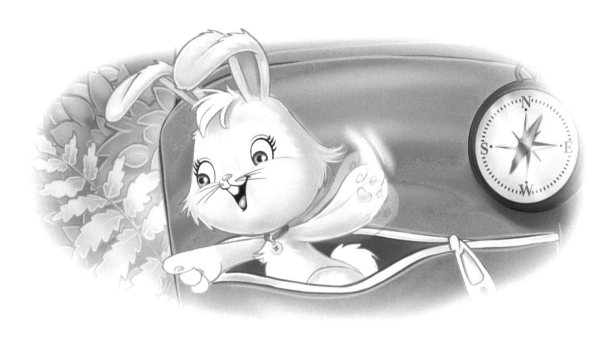

"...7...8...9...10!" Zozo opened her eyes and looked around. At first, she didn't see Tarrak. *He really is just like a shadow!* Zozo thought. After a while, though, she found Tarrak hiding among the low hanging branches of a tree. Zozo waved at him so he'd hide again.

"Oh, you found me!" Tarrak said. "Now watch me make like a river and run!" Then he went off to hide.

Zozo laughed at Tarrak's joke and closed her eyes to count again.

The second time Zozo looked for Tarrak was even harder than the first. But she finally found him hiding in a clump of bushes near the river. Zozo waved. Tarrak popped his head up and said, "I thought you'd never find me."

Zozo laughed again. This bear was fun and funny!

Tarrak and Zozo kept playing until the group stopped to rest. Still unnoticed by Zozo's family, Tarrak came over and gobbled down a few handfuls of blueberries. When he'd had his fill, he asked, "Instead of playing more hide-and-go-seek, will you swim with me? I'm hot and a little tired of hiding."

"I'm not sure," Zozo said hesitantly.

"I now know where we're going," Tarrak assured her. "I promise we'll stay close by your family, and it'll be fun!"

Zozo nodded and hopped onto Tarrak's back. Then Tarrak silently tiptoed into the river, as Zozo's family began the last stretch of their hike.

"Wow!" Zozo exclaimed as river water splashed onto her fur. "This water is ice cold!"

"Sure is," Tarrak said, "but do you know what's really cold?"

Zozo shook her head. "No. What?"

"Winter!" Tarrak laughed. "Here in Alaska, winter is very cold... and dark! Do you know why that's so great?" Tarrak asked but then immediately blurted out the answer before Zozo could say a word. "It's perfect for sleeping!" he said with a big, wide grin.

Zozo definitely liked that answer.

"When winter approaches," Tarrak continued, "it grows colder and darker. Bears like me crawl into our dens with a big belly full of food and stay tucked in all winter long. In spring, we come out to play and eat again."

"Sounds amazing!" Zozo said. "Who wouldn't love to crawl under the covers and stay comfy and warm for months and months?" Zozo smiled thinking of how fun it would be.

Thump, thump, thump. Again, Zozo heard the bears long before she saw them. "I hear your brothers," she said, listening to the sound of heavy feet pounding the beach.

"Me too," Tarrak said as he and Zozo finished swimming.

Dripping wet, Zozo and Tarrak climbed onto the
river's rocky banks and hugged each other goodbye.
Then, joking one last time, Tarrak turned and said,
"Watch me make like thunder and roll!" In an instant,
he'd somersaulted through the bushes toward his
brothers and was gone.

Soon Zozo's family appeared along the path. They
saw Tarrak and his brothers playing. Eager to watch
one last group of bears in the wild, Zozo's family
didn't notice when she slipped back into their group.

Before long, Zozo and her family were back in their kayaks, paddling toward the waiting floatplane. Zozo smiled, thinking about how bears *were* great and clever...and fun and funny...and so much more.

The floatplane's engine rumbled, and its front propeller whirled.
Zozo knew she'd miss the bears of Alaska, especially her friend
Tarrak. As the little plane rose above the bears' island home,
she looked back toward Tarrak. With a little giggle, she thought,
Watch me make like lightning and bolt!

Meet Zozo's new friends in the series' next adventure, Travels with Zozo... in the Fjord!

Travels with Zozo...and the Bears   by A.J. Atlas   illustrated by Anne Zimanski

Published by ImaginOn Books, an imprint of ImaginOn LLC
www.imaginonbooks.com

Copyright © 2022 by A.J. Atlas

1st Edition
2 4 6 8 10 9 7 5 3 1

978-1-954405-01-1 (Hardcover)   978-1-954405-31-8 (Ebook)

Printed in U.S.A.

To purchase books or obtain more information about the author, illustrator, or upcoming books, visit www.travelswithzozo.com

CPSIA information can be obtained
at www.ICGtesting.com
Printed in the USA
LVHW071127160622
721141LV00003B/4